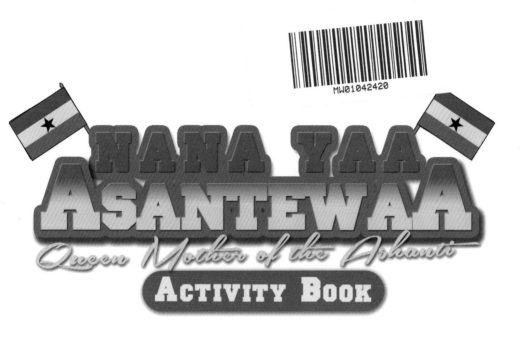

NANA YAA ASANTEWAA
Queen Mother of the Ashanti
ACTIVITY BOOK

Designed and Illustrated by
Andrew Lindo

Published 2019 by Black History Activity Books

Copyright @ Newborn Design

You'll find the answers and solutions to the puzzles on page 30.

BLACK HISTORY ACTIVITY BOOKS

Ashanti Empire

Of Ghana

NAME: _____

DATE OF BIRTH: _____

ADDRESS: _____

_____

_____

WHAT IS YOUR FAVOURITE ANIMAL?

_____

_____

SIGNATURE: _____

Yaa Asantewaa

Yaa Asantewaa was a Queen Mother of the Ashanti Empire and 'Protector of the Golden Stool'.

She was born on the 17th October 1840 in Southern Ghana.

Yaa Asantewaa is a true legend, known for her bravery, courage and fearlessness when fighting-off the British Army.

Yaa Asantewaa led the Ashanti into their final battle against the British in 1900. This was known as the War of the Golden Stool.

The Gold Coast of Ghana

Yaa Asantewaa was born in the heart of the Ashanti Empire in 1840. This part of the Ashanti empire is now a part of Central Ghana.

> This is the shape of Ghana.
>
> Can you find the shape and colour it in.

Clue: Ghana is in West Africa

Ashanti Kingdom

The Ashanti Empire was very large and it was known for its vast amounts of gold. Below is the Ashanti flag. In the middle of the flag is the 'Golden Stool' which is a symbol of unity and the soul of the Ashanti people.

Can you colour in flag of the Ashanti in neatly? Use the key code below.

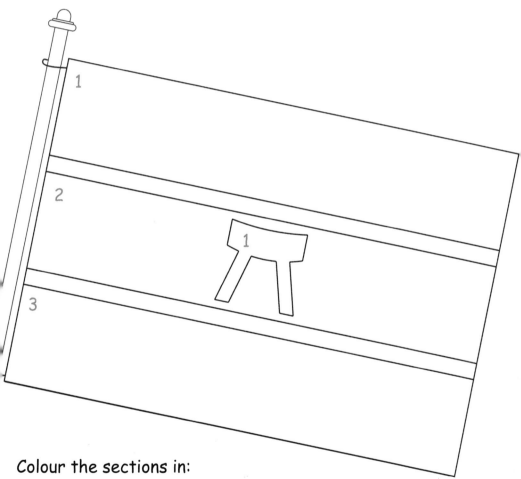

Colour the sections in:
1 = Yellow
2 = Black
3 = Green

Adinkra Symbols

The Ashanti people use symbols called 'Adinkra'.

Below are some adinkra symbols. Write the correct name next to the symbol.

Gye Nyame   Sankofa   Denkyem   Sesa wo suban   Aya   Akoma

Write The Name Below:

_____

_____

_____

_____

_____

_____

Akofena

Below is an Adinkra symbol for courage. This symbol was used to represent Nana Yaa Asantewaa.

See if you can connect the dots to form the Akofena.

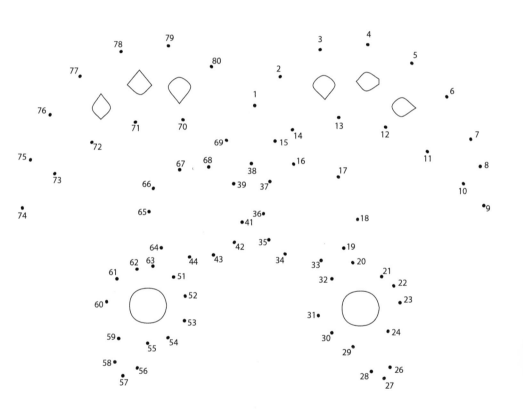

Symbol of The Ashanti

The porcupine is a symbol of the Ashanti people. The Ashanti nation's motto is "Kum apem a, apem beba" (stop a thousand, a thousand will rise). The Ashanti consider themselves to rise like the porcupine's spikes.

Can you count the number of spikes on these porcupines?

1.

This porcupine has _____ spikes.

2

This porcupine has _____ spikes.

3.

This porcupine has _____ spikes.

4.

This porcupine has _____ spikes.

5.

This porcupine has _____ spikes.

6.

This porcupine has _____ spikes.

The Art of Trading

The Ashanti people used gold shapes as an early form of money. Each shape had a different value based on it's weight.

Each of the symbols below are worth different amounts. Can you use the codes to solve the equations?

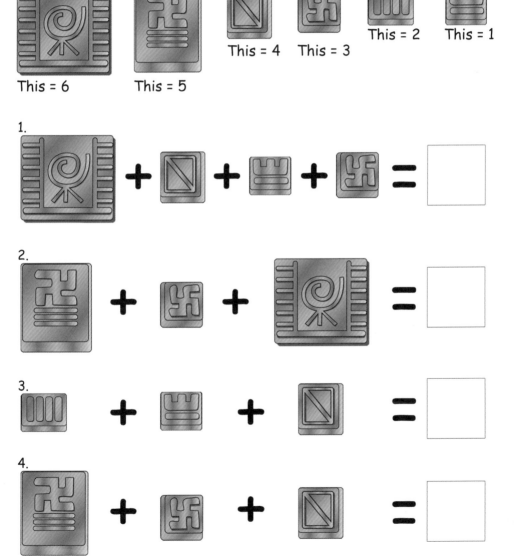

This = 6   This = 5   This = 4   This = 3   This = 2   This = 1

1.

⬚ + ⬚ + ⬚ + ⬚ = ☐

2.

⬚ + ⬚ + ⬚ = ☐

3.

⬚ + ⬚ + ⬚ = ☐

4.

⬚ + ⬚ + ⬚ = ☐

Defenders of The Golden Stool

The Golden Stool is the most sacred symbol to the Ashanti people. It is considered to be the heart of the Ashanti people as it holds all of the souls of the Ashanti.

See if you can connect the dots to form the Golden Stool.

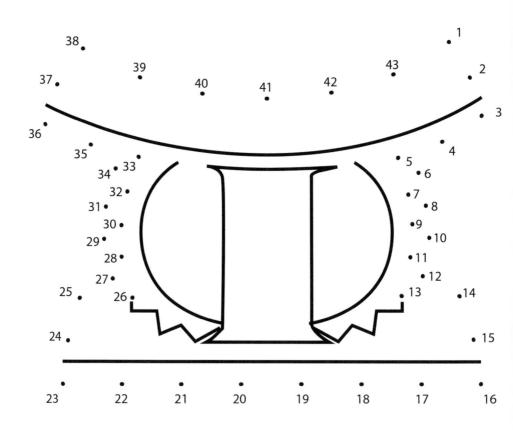

Okomfo Anokye

It is said that after prayers of the Ashanti high priest, Okomfo Anokye, the Golden Stool descended from heaven in a cloud of white dust and landed in the lap of the first Ashanti Emperor- Asantehene Osei Tutu.

Can you colour in this image of Okomfo Anokye receiving the Golden Stool?

Queen Mother of the Ashanti

In 1894, Yaa Asantewaa was crowned as Queen Mother of the Ashanti and defender of the 'Golden Stool'.

Can you colour in this picture of Yaa Asantewaa at her coronation?

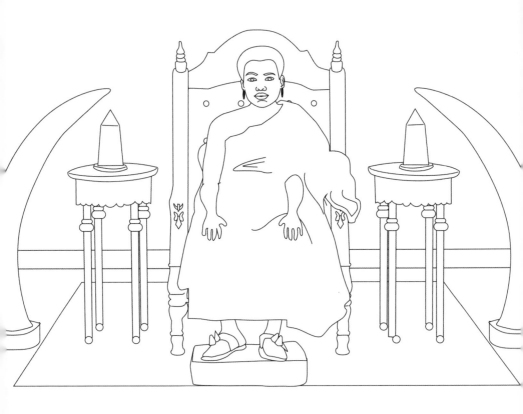

Meeting In Kumasi

After the British invaded Ghana they heard news about the Golden Stool. Greedy to get their hands on the Golden Stool, the British called a meeting with the Ashanti in the city of Kumasi.

Can you help Yaa Asantewaa find her way to Kumasi?

Start Here

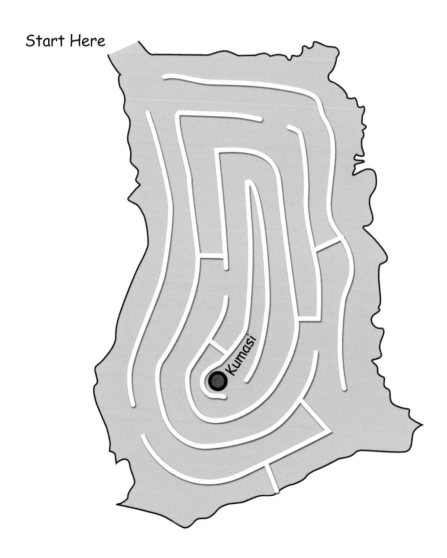

Fool's Gold

The British demanded that the Golden Stool be handed over to them. This made Yaa Asantewaa very angry so she had to think of a solution. She decided the British only wanted the Golden Stool for money and did not understand how sacred it was so she decided to make a fake stool and give it to the British.

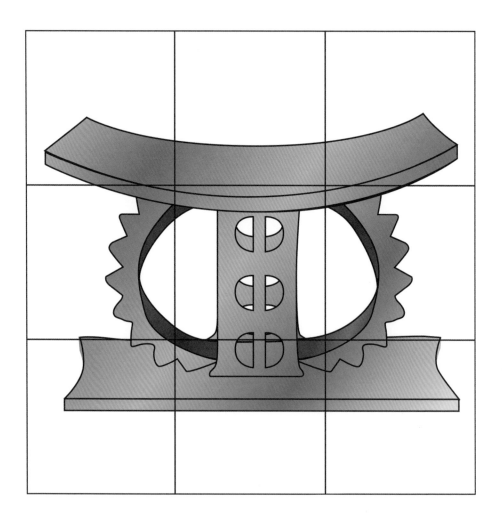

Square Grid

Create a fake stool to give to the British by copying the Golden Stool into the square grid below.

Don't forget to colour it in gold to fool the British!

War of The Golden Stool

When the British took the stool back home, they discovered that it was fake so they declared war with the Ashanti people. The British started the war of the Golden Stool so Yaa Ashantewaa had to prepare herself for war.

Spot The Difference

How many differences can you spot?

Clue: There are 22 altogether

Magical Amulets

Yaa Asantewaa's outfit for war was covered in magical amulets to protect her in battle.

Can you count the differenct types of amulets on this jacket and write the amount in the blank space below?

△ = _____ .

⊗ = _____ .

▨ = _____ .

✕ = _____ .

▮ = _____ .

Block the Fort

During the war, the Ashanti backed the British into a fort in Kumasi. The British decided to lock themselves in this fort. The walls of the fort were too thick to be penetrated so Yaa Asantewaa had to think of another way of getting in.

Can you place the blocks below into the correct spaces to form a blockade on the main door to the fort?

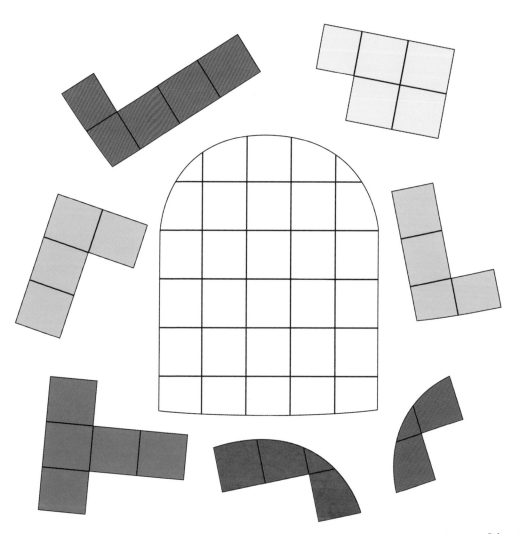

Road Block

Yaa Asantewaa blocked all of the roads going in and out of the fort. This stopped all food, ammunition and supplies getting to the British.

To the right is an example of a blockage with 5 layers. Can you draw the correct amount of layers across the blank walls to create a blockage on the roads?

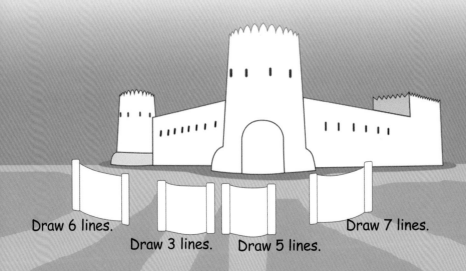

Draw 6 lines.

Draw 3 lines.

Draw 5 lines.

Draw 7 lines.

Secret message

After months of holding the British, Yaa Asantewaa decided to let women and sick people go but a secret message was sent from the fort calling for help.

Below is a secret code using adrinka symbols.
Can you use the code to find the words written below?

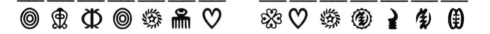

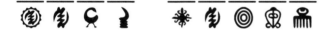

Exiled to the Seychelles

The British came back to Ghana with more reinforcements and captured Yaa Asantewaa and her only granddaughter. Yaa Asantewaa surrendered and was taken to the island of the Seychelles.

Can you find the correct route to the Seychelles?
The correct route is _____.

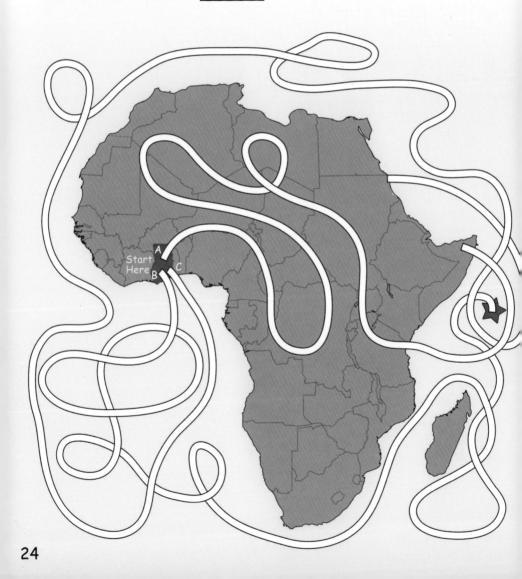

Always Victorious

Yaa Asantewaa was still victorious as the British never managed to get the Golden Stool.

Can you find the matching pair of Golden Stools by drawing a circle around them?

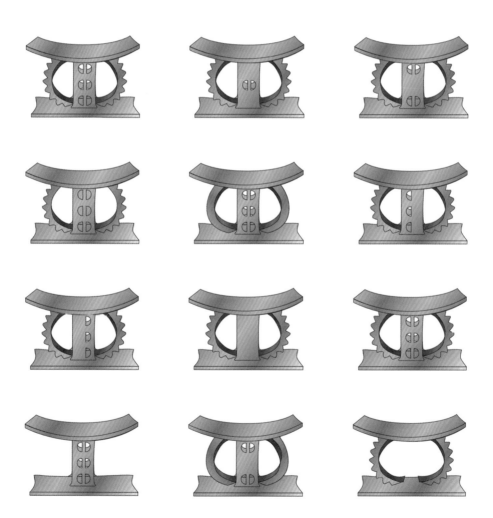

Key Words

The words below are related to Yaa Asantewaa. To help you learn the spelling of these words, copy the words in to the blank spaces.

<u>Copy The Words Here:</u>

1. Ashanti   _____ Ashanti _____

2. Empire   _____ Empire _____

3. Ghana   _____ Ghana _____

4. Kumasi   _____ Kumasi _____

5. Golden   _____ Golden _____

6. Stool   _____ Stool _____

7. Queen   _____ Queen _____

8. Nana   _____ Nana _____

9. Porcupine   _____ Porcupine _____

10. Adinkra   _____ Adinkra _____

11. Asantewaa   _____ Asantewaa _____

Word Search

```
L I N D O Z A N D R E W R Z
E M P I R E S A N K O F A Y
N P B S U M H T F G H A N A
S L S N A N A E R O A L I A
G B X A O I N Y G N R A S A
A O E A N H T R E O R N T S
Z S L I P K I F K O L T A A
T E G D E A O C U C O D N N
U Y R T E B M F M L R T C T
G C W E L N U M A W F I E E
Y H E A F R I Q S O R O Z W
E E A D K A S H I R E N Q A
N L M I A N T A L A E T E A
Y L E N N P O R C U P I N E
A E A K G S O R A T C N E W
M S F R O A L I V F O R T E
E M K A L F A H E R K H N A
A S A F R I C A N Q U E E N
R R C Y K A L B N G A R N W
E I O K O M F O A N O K Y E
```

☐ ASHANTI
☐ EMPIRE
☐ GHANA
☐ ADINKRA
☐ GYE NYAME
☐ SANKOFA
☐ GOLDEN
☐ STOOL
☐ PORCUPINE

☐ GOLD
☐ FORT
☐ NANA
☐ QUEEN
☐ KUMASI
☐ YAA ASANTEWAA
☐ OKOMFO ANOKYE
☐ AMULETS
☐ SEYCHELLES
☐ AFRICA

> Please help me find these words. You can tick the boxes as you find them.

The Legend

Yaa Asantewaa lead the last war against the British in Ghana. Her spirit will forever live on.

Can you colour in the picture of Yaa Asantewaa in her war uniform?

Quiz

Now that you have completed this book, let's see how much you have learnt about Yaa Astantewaa by answering the following questions.

1. Where was Yaa Asantewaa born?
   a. Congo ☐   b. America ☐   c. Ghana ☐

2. What was the name of Yaa Astantewaa's people?
   a. Imbangala ☐   b. Ashanti ☐   c. Bantu ☐

3. What was Yaa Asantewaa a defender of?
   a. The Golden Calf ☐   b. The Golden Stool ☐
   c. The Golden Fist ☐

4. What animal is a symbol of the Ashanti People?
   a. Porcupine ☐   b. Lion ☐   c. Rhino ☐

5. What is the name of the symbols the Ashanti use?
   a. Hieroglyphics ☐   b. Emojis ☐   c. Adinkra ☐

6. What country wanted the Golden Stool?
   a. America ☐   b. Great Britain ☐   c. France ☐

7. What are your favourite things about Yaa Astantewaa?

_____

_____

_____

_____

_____

Answers

Page 7

Page 10

1 = 4
2 = 6
3 = 7
4 = 10
5 = 14
6 = 20

Page 11

1 = 14
2 = 14
3 = 7
4 = 12

Page 15

Page 19

Page 20

 = 10

= 4

= 3

= 9

 = 7

Page 21

Page 23

Ashanti Kingdom

Gold Coast

Ghana

Golden Stool

Porcupine

Page 24

Page 25

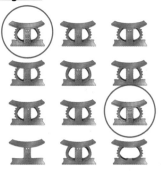

Page 27

Page 29

1 = c,   2 = b,   3 = b,   4 = a,   5 = c,   6 = b